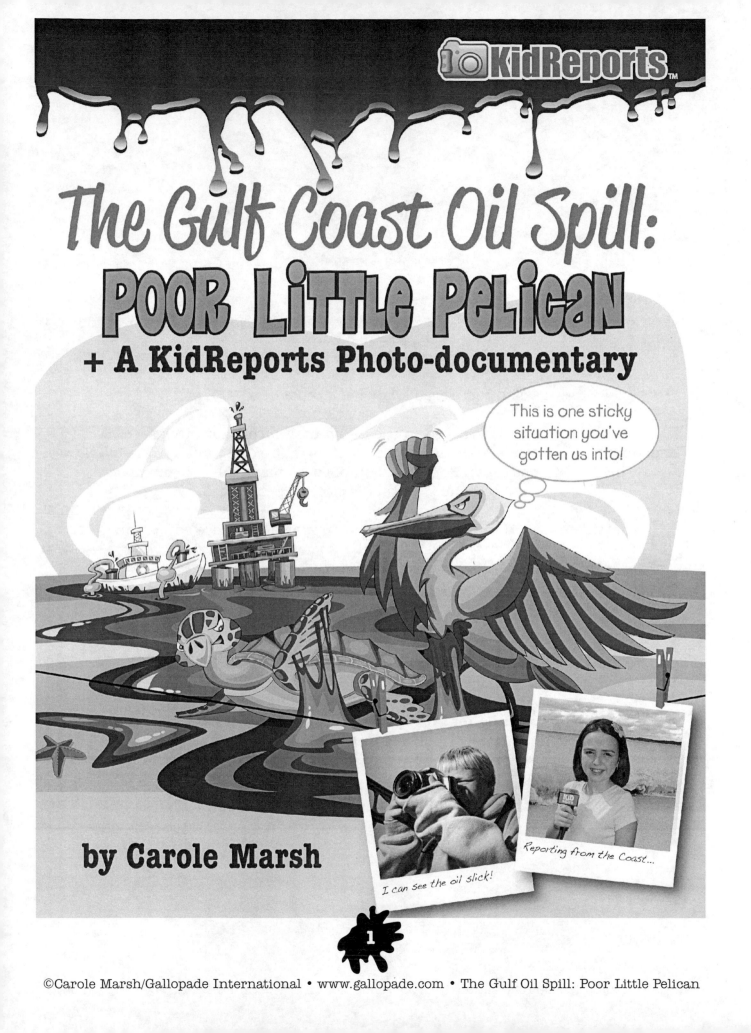

Published by

GALLOPADE
INTERNATIONAL

800-536-2438
www.gallopade.com

Graphic Design, Vicki DeJoy   Story Illustrations, Jessica Talley
Editor, Paige Muh
KidReporter for this book: Erin Lamb

Dawn® is a registered trademark of Procter & Gamble

Gallopade is proud to be a member and supporter of these educational
organizations and associations:

Association for the Study of African American Life and History
National Alliance of Black School Educators
American Booksellers Association
American Library Association
International Reading Association
National Association for Gifted Children
The National School Supply and Equipment Association
The National Council for the Social Studies
Museum Store Association
Association of Partners for Public Lands
Association of Booksellers for Children

In 2010, there was an oil rig accident in the Gulf
which caused the release of millions of gallons of oil.
This oil spill came ashore into many marshes,
wetlands, and on to beaches, affecting the fishing and tourism
industries, and most especially, the fragile coastal environment and the
creatures who make their home there. The clean-up continues.
The long-term consequences are not known.

The Gulf Coast Oil Spill: POOR Little PeliCan
+ A KidReports Photo-documentary

Hi, I'm Erin and I'm here
to give you a KIDREPORT of what
happened along the Gulf Coast. We kids care
about our environment and the creatures
who share it with us, don't we?
I think you'll enjoy this book and learn a lot
because here's what's inside!...

SOME PEOPLE
CALLED
THE OIL SPILL...
A CRUDE
AWAKENING!

3

An original short story by my favorite author, Carole Marsh. It's called **The Poor Little Pelican**. You'll meet some pretty neat pelicans and easily imagine what it must have been like when the Dark Shadow of oil came ashore! It starts on page 5.

Also, all along the way, I'll join in to share:

- A map of the Gulf Coast, page 21
- All about the oil spill, what it meant, and what kids did to help, pages 22-25
- A list of birds, fish, and other animals affected, page 27
- Questions and Answers about the oil spill, pages 31-33
- A Gulf Coast Glossary, pages 34-35

AND LOTS OF PICTURES AND ART!

Carole Marsh at the beach!

So, come on in—the water's fine!
No, really, the water is fine!
Let's learn together
and have a good time.

ECOSYSTEM:
THE SYSTEM FORMED BY A COMMUNITY OF ANIMALS AND THEIR INTERACTION WITH THEIR ENVIRONMENT

4

POOR Little PeLicaN
...and the DaRk ShaDOW

5

"If anyone can, a Pelican!" Pristina Pelican always said. She was the grandmother of a clan of pelicans that had lived along the lovely Gulf Coast of America for a long time.

Pristina was very old, but she was very wise. Protractor, her son, was old, but still a strong flier. Both of them had seen many changes along the lovely Gulf Coast during their lives. They had many pelican friends from Texas to Louisiana to Alabama to Mississippi to Florida.

Petrus was a young pelican. While he had respect for his elders, he was adventuresome, daring, and, sometimes, foolhardy. Since he liked to have company on his outings, he often coaxed his younger sister, Priscilla, into tagging along. She loved adventure, too, but she was more cautious, although she could seldom convince her rambunctious older brother to calm down and listen to her.

"Let's go!" Petrus pleaded one lovely Gulf morning. "The sky is blue, the air clear, the water whipping up whitecaps. Besides, I'm hungry, and I smell fish!"

Priscilla laughed. "All you think of is eating, big brother! But let's head out and fill your bill and your belly. I, myself, sense a storm coming on, so I suppose we should get you fed in case we have to hunker down in the marsh for awhile."

Yes, Priscilla was always cautious. Petrus was always hungry. And they had been taught well by their grandmother and father. They were smart young pelicans and knew the ways of the winged world, and so off they flew delighted with the day and an adventure ahead.

Out over the glistening Gulf waters, the two pelicans first flew high, spying the sparkling sand of the coastline like a long, scrawled signature. Then they flew low, their large brown bodies almost hugging the waves just beneath them. Their keen eyes scoured the water, their large beaks ready to blossom open as soon as...

7

8

"Fish!" cried Petrus and struck quick and sure.
With one gulp his joyful feeding frenzy had begun.

Priscilla laughed as she drafted her brother, flying
close in formation behind him, innately graceful,
as opposed to her brother who flew a bit helter-
skelter over the waves, determined not to miss a
good catch.

Priscilla loved to enjoy the breathtaking view of
the blue Gulf waters, the white eyebrows of barrier
islands, the elegant strands of marsh, the sandy
shore with little candy-colored homes all in a row,
and often, those cute little children staring and
pointing at her and her brother as they flew
overhead.

Sometimes, other pelicans joined them in their
sky-high ballet as they showed off their ability to
swoop, sway, dive, and thrive on the bounty of
the sea. But this day, Priscilla had no appetite.
She just had a funny feeling that something was
not right.

9

Soon she spotted the large black thing jutting out of the water that she always found so curious. It was not a house. It was not a boat. It was not even a seaplane. It bobbed precariously. A few men could sometimes be seen working on the black thing. Usually it seemed harmless, but today Priscilla noticed that the structure rocked more than usual, and a large shadow, not caused by a cloud overhead or a school of fish below, bubbled and blossomed ominously beneath the water.

As Petrus flew on, filling his beak so full that an occasional lucky fish found overboard escape, Priscilla swooped lower to examine the black shadow that was growing ever larger. She did not understand what it was, but she did not like the look of it. No, she did not like it at all. Suddenly, Petrus swooped by. "Let's head home, sister. I am so full!"

"It's all about you, isn't it, big brother?" Priscilla

10

teased. She followed her brother, eager to ask father and grandmother if they knew what caused such a Dark Shadow under the sea.

"I've seen the Dark Shadow before," father explained when Petrus and Priscilla returned home to their nest.

"What is it?" asked Petrus. "Is it ink of the octopus?"

"No," said father. "It is not ink of the octopus."

"Is it pluff mud?" Priscilla guessed.

"No, it is not pluff mud," said father.

Grandmother looked very somber. She had seen the Dark Shadow before, as well. "Tell them," she said, shaking her head sadly.

Father sighed. "The Dark Shadow is...oil," he said.

"Oil?" said Petrus. "I have never seen that creature."

11

"Oil?" pondered Priscilla. "What is that?"

"Oil is a natural substance," father explained. "It is usually hidden deep within the earth. But humans want and need oil, so they build big drilling rigs in the sea and punch into the earth until they find oil, then pump it out."

"Do they eat it?" asked Priscilla.

"Can we eat it?!" Petrus asked hopefully.

Grandmother shook her head. "It is for fuel, but it is not to eat. It is used in human's machines—automobiles, they call them."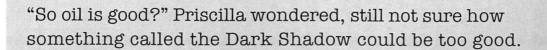

"So oil is good?" Priscilla wondered, still not sure how something called the Dark Shadow could be too good.

"Oil is not bad," said father, "but it is not good when it escapes into the water, and then washes into the marshes."

"Is that what the Dark Shadow that we saw today is doing?" asked Petrus.

"I'm afraid so," said father.

"I am very afraid so," agreed grandmother.

Petrus and Priscilla did not understand.

The next morning Petrus and Priscilla were up early. They headed to sea, to fly over the Gulf waters and see if they could spot the Dark Shadow again. They did, only now the Dark Shadow was much bigger and much wider, much darker, and much deeper.

Suddenly, Petrus spied a place where the Dark Shadow was washing to shore. "Look!" he told Priscilla. "Let's go down and see what the Dark Shadow is doing on the shore. Maybe we can taste it. Maybe it is good."

"Maybe it is bad," Priscilla said. "Or dangerous." But she followed Petrus through the sky. As they flew exuberantly over the waves and landed on the shore, they spotted a...a...well, they were not sure what it was.

13

"What is that?" asked Petrus, padding toward the curious creature.

"It looks familiar," said Priscilla. "It looks like...like...us!"

"No it doesn't," said Petrus. "Or maybe it does," he added thoughtfully. "Only it is covered in mud."

As they got closer to the creature, Priscilla corrected her brother. "Not mud," she said quietly, "oil."

Sure enough, the young pelican they came upon was so covered in thick, black oil that it looked like a Dark Shadow of itself. Petrus and Priscilla tried to talk to the young pelican, but it could hardly move, it was so covered in oil, much less speak. It could not ruffle its feathers. It could not fly. It looked so sad.

"Poor little pelican!" Priscilla said, rushing to the bird. "What happened to you?"

14

"The oil," said the little pelican. "It washed ashore and now I am covered in it. So are my friends."

Priscilla and Petrus glanced around and spotted nearby fish and crabs and other beach creatures also covered with oil from the Dark Shadow. They realized that the green grasses of the marsh were also now brown and dirty and that the usually snow white beach was now grimy and black. It was very ugly, very smelly, and very bad.

"What can we do to help?" begged Priscilla.

"Nothing," said the poor little pelican sadly. "Nothing."

Then suddenly, two humans, a tall girl and a short boy, came running toward the birds.

"Quick, fly!" warned Priscilla, and she and Petrus took flight and landed a short distance away in safety. "Come on, little pelican, fly! Fly!" they pleaded back to their new oil-covered friend. But the little pelican's feathers were so saturated with the oil that it could not fly. It could not even try.

15

Soon the girl and boy reached the little pelican and hovered over it. Priscilla was so scared! What were they doing to the poor little pelican? The children were between the little pelican and Priscilla and Petrus, who just cowered in the marsh and watched carefully, ready to come to the aid of their new little friend as soon as it was safe. Soon, the boy and girl moved, and Petrus and Priscilla were astounded. Instead of the poor little pelican, they saw a clean fluffy little pelican. As the children hurried off, Petrus and Priscilla flew to the pelican. "What happened to you?" they asked.

"They cleaned off the oil!" said the little pelican. "And look! Now they are cleaning my friends!"

The pelicans could see the children scampering from creature to creature, using foamy white soap and a soft brush to wash the oil off of crabs, otters, rabbits, turtles, seabirds, and other coastal critters as quickly and gently as they could.

"Much better!" said Petrus.
"Much better!" said Priscilla.

17

"But what happened to us?" asked the poor little pelican. "And why?"

"It was the Dark Shadow," Priscilla explained. "Our father said that humans let it escape into the waters and now it is coming ashore. They are trying to clean it up, but it is taking time."

The poor little pelican looked sad. "I know. Not all my friends have been as lucky as me to have some kids come clean them up. Those humans, they should be more careful."

Petrus said, "It is still very early and I am so hungry. Do you think you could fly with us and get some breakfast?"

The little pelican ruffled its feathers. "Yes, I think I can!"

18

"Good!" said Priscilla. "Let's go!"

The trio of pelicans took flight. Out over the blue Gulf waters they flew in formation, keeping a keen eye out for fish in the waves. As they flew into the sunrise, they did not see the Dark Shadow plume of oil growing and growing, spreading far and wide into the pristine marshes and crystal white shore. And, on to any creatures in its dark path.

In the distance, on the shore, the children ran more quickly than ever from creature to creature, trying to clean as many as they could.

The eND?

19

In April 2010, there was an oil rig accident in the Gulf
which caused the release of millions of gallons of oil.
This oil spill came ashore into many marshes, wetlands,
and on to beaches, affecting the fishing and tourism industries,
and most especially, the fragile coastal environment
and the creatures who make their home there.
In September, the leaking oil well was permanently sealed.

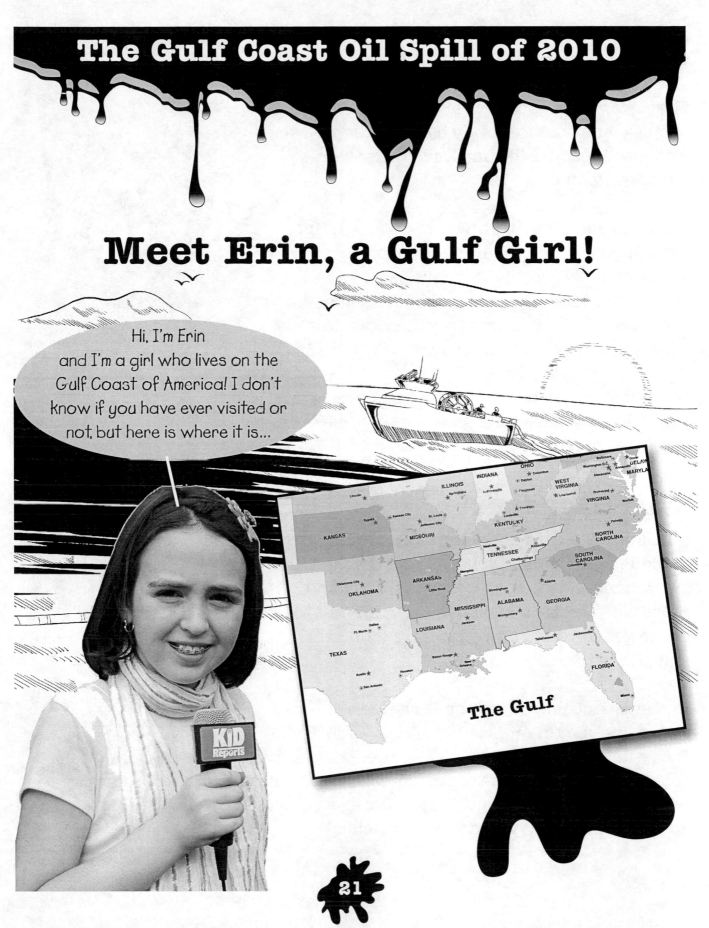

Most of the time, the Gulf Coast is a place of white sand, green wetlands, and blue waters. These waters and wetlands are very important. They are where gobs of creatures live. Also, many people come here for lovely beach vacations. And lots of people, like my Dad, make their living by fishing.

If you go out in our Gulf Waters, you will find fishing boats. You might also spy oil rigs. These are tall platforms where people live and work while they pump oil up from beneath the water. This oil is sent to refineries and ends up as gas in our cars and trucks.

Fishing boats

Most of the time this oil-getting-business works just fine. But if there is some kind of "mess up" it can create an oil spill. That is not good!

The Disaster!

Oil-covered pelican

On April 20, 2010, an oil rig in the Gulf exploded and sank. Oil began to spew from the earth beneath the sea. Because the rig and pipes were destroyed, it was very difficult to try to get the oil to stop. It took a lot of work and a long time.

In the meantime, oil was spilling into the water and making its way to shore. Unfortunately, many fish, birds, and other creatures were either covered in oil or maybe drank some of it. Needless to say, this is not good for them! It was also not good for the water, wetlands, or beaches!

22

What To Do?

Very quickly, everyone went to work to try to stop the flow of oil by plugging the oil pipe. Other people worked hard to try to skim the oil out of the water. Some people put up "booms" to try to prevent the oil from coming ashore in wetlands or on beaches. And even other people cleaned birds and other shore creatures by giving them a good bath!

Some of these efforts worked. Others did not work as good. Also, a big storm came up and sort of messed up being out in the water for awhile. Days, weeks, then months went by. In the meantime, more oil was coming ashore. It made what they call "tar balls" on the beaches. People went out and picked them up. Everyone went on cleaning everything they could. The pipe letting the oil out was finally stopped. But it still takes a long time to clean up such a big mess!

Those doggone tar balls!

OIL SPIL AREA CLOS NO WATER CONT

No swimming today—phooey!

Oil booms

23

In the Meantime...

In the meantime, some other bad things were happening. Because of the oil, a lot of places fishermen like my Dad work were put "off limits." This meant that many, many fishermen in the Gulf were out of work. It was not clear when they would be allowed to fish again. Everyone wondered if all the fish would die. Would they be toxic because of the oil? It was a difficult time with a lot of worry.

It was also summer when the Gulf is usually covered not in oil, but in TOURISTS! When a lot of people worried that the beaches would be all nasty, they changed their plans and did not come to the Gulf Coast. This made it hard on families who make their living by renting hotel rooms or cottages, or feeding tourists, and things like that.

Oil!

24

What Kids Did!

As you might imagine, we Gulf Coast kids cared a lot about the oil spill and what it was doing to our land and water. We felt sorry for families whose Dad or Mom could no longer work at their jobs.

We asked, "What can we kids do?!" Soon, we found ourselves busy helping in all kinds of ways, but what we liked best was to help any animals or sea creatures or birds. It was sad to see the ones affected by the oil, but it was exciting to help many of them get clean and better.

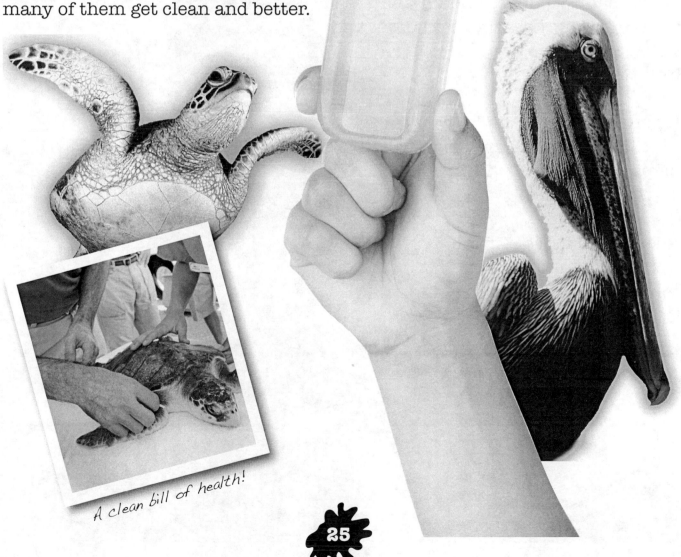

No soap in my eyes, please!

A clean bill of health!

25

What's Next?

As you can also imagine, this is a disaster that did not just go away overnight. It will take a long time for the oil to get out of the water...to get cleaned up in the wetlands...to get picked up off the beaches. It will take a long time for all the jobs that were lost to come back. Maybe some jobs never will?

I know it will take a long time for those of us who live here to forget about the oil spill. We just hope it never happens again. My Dad said good things often come out of bad things. So I hope we learn how to avoid such a terrible oil spill. I know that my family, friends, and I really appreciate our beautiful Gulf Coast and want it to always be clean and beautiful and safe.

When I grow up, I think I would like to study hard and have a job that helps the coastal environment and all who live there!

Also, I would love it if you would come and visit sometime. The Gulf is...GREAT!

26

Gulf Coast Animals and the Oil Spill

Of all the questions kids have about the oil spill, most are about the animals, right?

Here are just some of the creatures affected by the oil spill:

Brown pelicans
White pelicans
Laughing gulls
Herring gulls
Northern gannets
Night herons
Cattle egrets
Snowy egrets
Reddish egrets
Least bitterns

Caspian terns
Common terns
Royal terns
Sandwich terns
Least terns
White ibis
Dunlins
Roseate spoonbills
Sanderlings
Terrapins

King snake
American oystercatcher
Wilson's plover
Snowy plover
Mottled duck
Clapper rail
Black rail
Seaside sparrow
Dolphins
Sperm whales

And don't forget oysters, sharks, bluefin tuna, sea turtles, songbirds, and many, many more marine creatures that can be badly affected by oil!

27

How do the animals get so covered in oil?

When they dive into the water for food or when they land on beaches, oil can get on their feathers. Sea turtles and dolphins can get oil on them when they come to the surface of the water to breathe.

What does the oil do to the creatures? When birds try to clean their feathers, oil can get in their beaks and they swallow it. Oil can also hurt their eyes and lungs. Chemicals in the oil can harm fish and birds. Small creatures such as shrimp, crabs, oysters, or turtle hatchlings can be hurt or even killed by oil or the chemicals in it. Chemicals can be toxic, or poisonous. Think of the water from top to bottom. Think of the water all the way to the land. All creatures who live or travel through can be affected by the oil spill.

Most kids think that if the animals are cleaned, they will be all right. Many times, that is true. But sometimes, animals die before they can be found and cleaned. Sometimes, they get cleaned but are too sick to survive. Tiny creatures have a really hard time recovering from the effects of oil. And even if an animal does not get oil on it, it might breathe, eat, or otherwise be affected by oil.

28

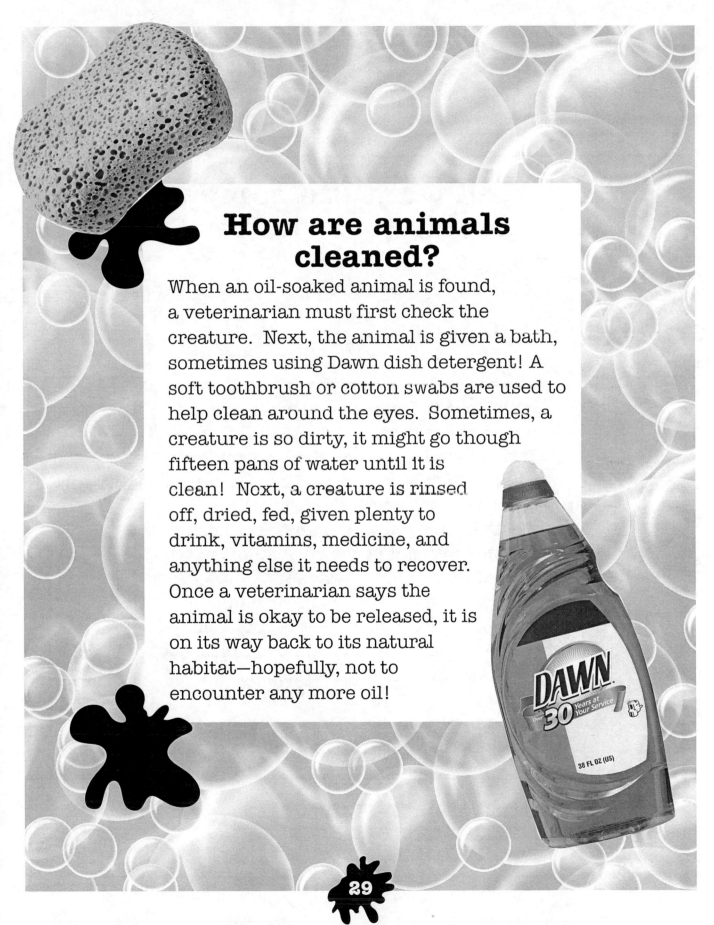

How are animals cleaned?

When an oil-soaked animal is found, a veterinarian must first check the creature. Next, the animal is given a bath, sometimes using Dawn dish detergent! A soft toothbrush or cotton swabs are used to help clean around the eyes. Sometimes, a creature is so dirty, it might go though fifteen pans of water until it is clean! Next, a creature is rinsed off, dried, fed, given plenty to drink, vitamins, medicine, and anything else it needs to recover. Once a veterinarian says the animal is okay to be released, it is on its way back to its natural habitat—hopefully, not to encounter any more oil!

29

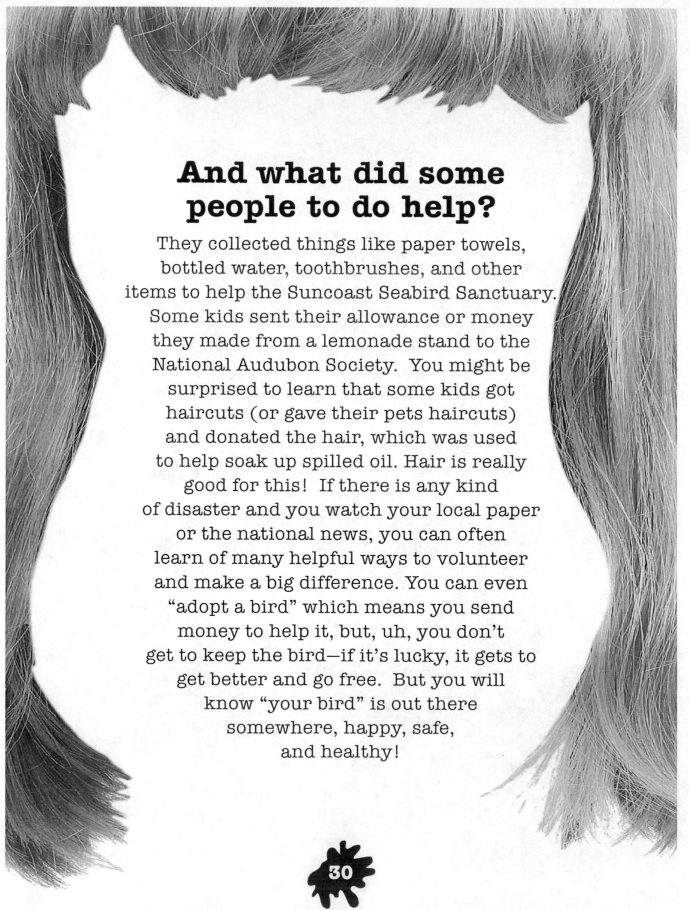

And what did some people to do help?

They collected things like paper towels, bottled water, toothbrushes, and other items to help the Suncoast Seabird Sanctuary. Some kids sent their allowance or money they made from a lemonade stand to the National Audubon Society. You might be surprised to learn that some kids got haircuts (or gave their pets haircuts) and donated the hair, which was used to help soak up spilled oil. Hair is really good for this! If there is any kind of disaster and you watch your local paper or the national news, you can often learn of many helpful ways to volunteer and make a big difference. You can even "adopt a bird" which means you send money to help it, but, uh, you don't get to keep the bird—if it's lucky, it gets to get better and go free. But you will know "your bird" is out there somewhere, happy, safe, and healthy!

30

Oil Spill Questions and Answers!

Can the waters and wetlands heal themselves?

As a matter of fact, fast-growing marshland appears to rid itself of oil in just a few months. Microbes actually "chew up" much of the oil on the surface, Mother Nature's way of helping take care of human's errors. Much of the oil has evaporated from the water or naturally dispersed into the seawater. This does not include all the work that was done to stop the oil flow and clean up the initial spill.

Wetland habitat

What about the animals? How will long term effects of the oil spill affect them?

Only time, and scientists, can tell just how well sea, land, and airborne life fares after the oil is gone. While most things may return to normal, it is possible that some life suffers longer term consequences of the oil or the dispersants that were used to help remove the oil. It is certain that many people will closely watch and be ready to help such creatures get back to normal as much as possible and as soon as possible.

Looking good!

31

How about people who live there or eat seafood from the Gulf?

Yes, many people who live and work in the Gulf Coast area have been affected by the oil spill. Some fishermen are back at work. Some fishing grounds that were closed have been reopened. Seafood is tested to make sure it is safe to eat. Beaches have been cleaned and tourists have returned to the Gulf Coast.

Will there ever be another oil spill in the Gulf?

Let's hope not! As you might imagine, everyone charged with keeping an eye on oil rigs, drilling for oil, and everything else that could lead to an oil spill is looking really hard and watching with very keen eyes to see that every precaution is taken to make sure that such a spill does not happen again. Oil spills do happen. Some are small and some are very large. But when bad things happen we often "learn lessons" that we can use to prevent such things from happening in the future.

32

Oil Spill Questions and Answers!

Will everything ever be back to normal?

Hopefully, it is believed that a full recovery from the effects of the oil spill may take years, instead of decades, which is good news.

Now that the oil spill is pretty much over, what can kids do to help?

I have a great answer for that! You can study hard! You might chose a career in environmental sciences so that one day you can grow up and help keep the Earth and its land, seas, skies, and creatures healthy and well. There are all kinds of jobs, whether in the legal profession, government, sciences, and other areas that can help. You could even become a writer and help others understand what is going on and what progress is being made in our environment. In the meantime, read and listen to the news and stay aware of what is happening in your area, region, nation, and around the world. It is a small world, after all, and what happens one place often affects others far away. Instead of being part of a problem, you can be part of a solution!

33

Oil Spill Glossary

barrier islands: narrow strips of sand "offshore" that help protect beaches from harsh wind, waves, and perhaps some oil

beaches: the sandy part of the shore from where the waves come ashore to where regular land begins

booms: artificial barriers put in the water to try to protect wetlands or beaches from oil spills

coastland: the entire coastal environment from the water, islands, beaches, wetlands, and inland

dispersant: natural or chemical additives used to help soak up or do away with oil

environment: all the land, water, air, and nature that make up a particular place such as the Gulf Coast

fishing industry: all the people, boats, places, and processes that are required from protecting fishing grounds to catching, processing, and delivering fish and other seafood products

habitat: the home or place where particular types of birds, animals, and fish live

hatchlings: the just born, very young of some types of creatures, such as sea turtles; because hatchlings are so small and immature they are especially vulnerable to any trouble in their environment

marshes: the grasses that grow between the water and the solid land; they often serve as a "filter" system to wash out bad things from that environment, but they are fragile and can be destroyed

34

Oil Spill Glossary

microbes: invisible except with a microscope "germs" some of which are very helpful in cleaning up oil

oil: a natural substance in nature that can be processed and become fuel for our gas tanks and for other uses

oil industry: the entire group of companies, people, places, processes, and more that makes up the worldwide business of finding, getting, processing, transporting, selling, and using oil and oil products

oil rig: a large metal structure where workers live and work while they drill for oil; what you see above the water is just part of an oil rig

tourism: the entire industry of travel, lodging, restaurants, advertising, and more that makes up the business of attracting visitors to a place and then serving their needs while they are there

toxic: something bad or poisonous, unhealthy, dangerous

veterinarian: a special doctor for animals who gives them "check-ups" and helps them with treatment and medications when needed

wetlands: the coastal environment of sand, water, trees, shrubs, and more that makes up a big, and protective, part of the area near bodies of water

35

What Does the Future Hold?

Should we be discouraged about the Gulf Coast oil disaster? Of course, but we should not be defeated! In addition to all the human efforts and scientific solutions that have helped to improve the situation, Mother Nature and time will help too.

After another large oil spill in Alaska, everyone wondered if things would ever be the same again. It takes time, but nature can also help to heal itself. Of course it would be better to never have an oil spill. It is hoped that with better laws and timely oversight of oil rigs, we can prevent such disastrous spills.

In the meantime, once all the "poor little pelicans" are washed, what can you do? You can study hard in school! You can learn about habitats and ecosystems. You might even want to consider a career in marine sciences, or waterways conservation, or habitat protection, or others, where you can grow up and make a difference. After all, the Gulf Coast and other waters of the world belong to you, and you will want them to be safe and clean for your children and grandchildren!

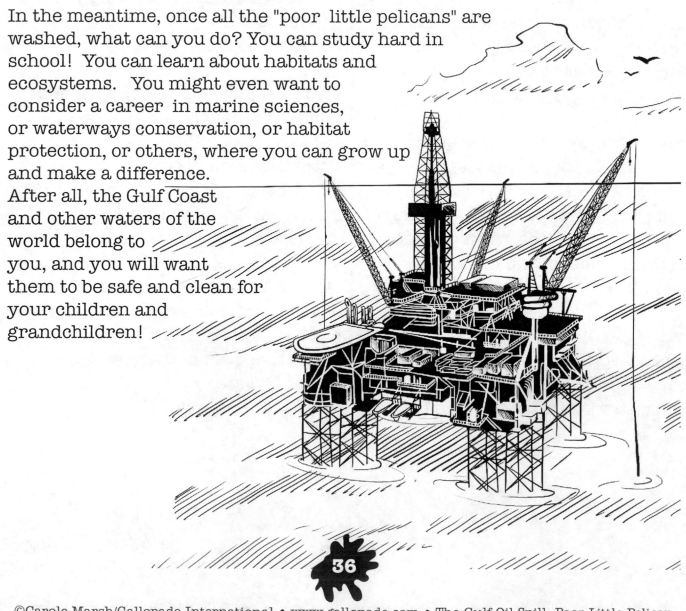

36